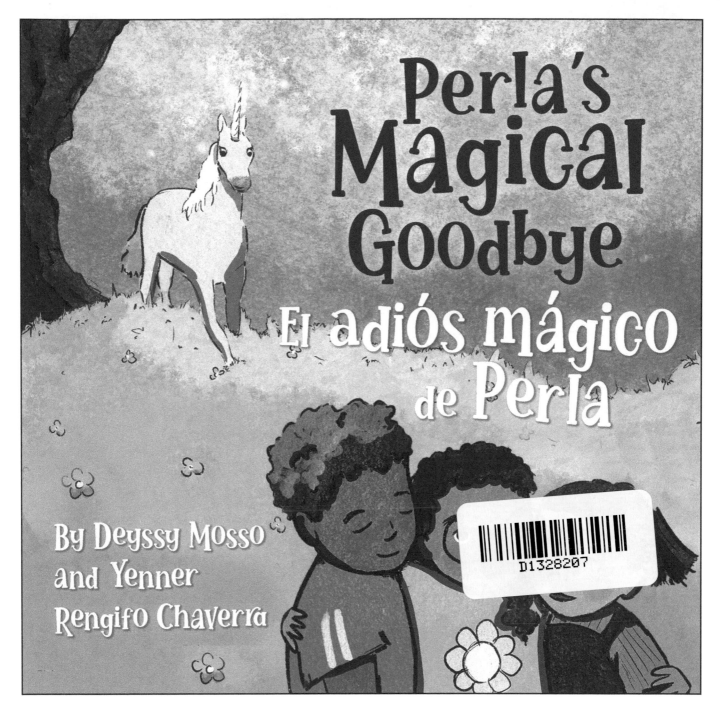

Perla's Magical Goodbye

El adiós mágico de Perla

By Deyssy Mosso and Yenner Rengifo Chaverra

Latin American Youth Center | Washington, DC

Shout Mouse Press

**Latin American Youth Center/
Shout Mouse Press**

Text copyright © 2021 by
Shout Mouse Press

Illustrations copyright © 2021
by Fatima Seck

Design by Amber Colleran

Spanish translation by
Tatiana Figueroa Ramirez and Ártemis López

ISBN: 978-1-950807-40-6

Shout Mouse Press is a nonprofit writing and
publishing program dedicated to amplifying
underheard voices. Learn more and see our
full catalog at www.shoutmousepress.org.

Shout Mouse Press
1638 R Street NW Suite 218
Washington, DC 20009

Trade distribution:
Ingram Book Group

For information about special discounts
and bulk purchases, please contact
Shout Mouse Press sales at 240-772-1545
or orders@shoutmousepress.org.

Acknowledgments

At Shout Mouse Press, we invite young people to write diverse and inclusive stories inspired by their own lived experiences. We believe that all children should be able to see themselves in the books they read, and that all children benefit from reading diverse perspectives on our shared world.

This book, written by young people from the Latin American Youth Center in Washington, DC, is born of this mission. These youth authors, ages 16-22, worked in teams of two to four to compose original children's books centering the hopes, dreams, joys, and challenges of being a young immigrant. They put their own hearts—and their personalities!—on the page, writing stories they hoped would inspire young readers to embrace who they are and to value the unique stories each one of us has to tell. These authors have our immense gratitude and respect: Mario, Jamileth, Tseganesh, Joy, Deyssy, Yenner, Andy, Marisol, Pedro, and Yunior.

This project represents a collaboration between Shout Mouse Press and the Latin American Youth Center (LAYC). From LAYC: Thanks to Cheili Obregon-Molina and Arisleidy Aquino for essential translation, collaboration, and positive energy, and to the LAYC program leadership of Julia Kann and Mike Leon. From Shout Mouse Press: We thank Programs Manager Alexa Patrick; Story Coaches Faith Campbell, Tatiana Figueroa Ramirez, and Barrett Smith; and Author Liaisons Rosa Reyes, Saylenis Palmore, Josselyn Mendoza, and Brenda Romero Peña for bringing fun and insight to the project. We can't thank enough illustrators Joy Ingram, Yurieli Otero-Asmar, Fatima Seck, and Ian Springer for bringing these stories to life with their beautiful artwork, and Amber Colleran for bringing a keen eye and important mentorship to the project as the series Art Director. Also muchísimas gracias are in order for Tatiana Figueroa Ramirez and Ártemis López for their thoughtful translation. We are grateful for the time and talents of these writers, mentors, and artists!

Finally, we are grateful to Today At Apple® Creative Studios DC, whose support made this project possible.

This book is dedicated to all children who have immigrated and had to leave their friends and family behind. May their memories and love stay with you.

Este libro está dedicado a todos los niños que han inmigrado y han tenido que dejar atrás a sus amistades y familiares. Que sus recuerdos y amor se queden con ustedes.

Perla and her friends Genesis and Pablo had always been together.

They lived in the town of San Unicornio, where everyone knew everyone else. All the kids went to the same school, all the families went to the same church, and everyone believed in the magical tale of the unicorn. Especially Perla.

Perla y sus amigos Génesis y Pablo siempre han estado juntos.

Vivían en el pueblo de San Unicornio, donde todos se conocían. Todos los niños iban a la misma escuela, todas las familias iban a la misma iglesia, y todos creían en la leyenda mágica del unicornio. Especialmente Perla.

Perla and her friends all loved magic. They loved to play games, too. They played soccer in the meadows, hide and seek in the trees, and make believe by the river.

Perla thought she'd always be by her friends' side. But that was about to change... because Perla was moving.

Perla y sus amigos amaban la magia. También amaban jugar. Jugaban al fútbol en el campo, a las escondidas en los árboles y jugaban a imaginar al lado del río.

Perla pensó que siempre estaría junto a sus amigos. Pero eso estaba a punto de cambiar... porque Perla se iba a mudar.

In fact, Perla was moving to a land far away, where none of them had ever been: America. She was going to leave her beloved grandma and go live with her parents. She was excited, but also sad.

De hecho, Perla se mudaba a una tierra muy lejana, donde ninguno de ellos había estado anteriormente: Norte América. Dejaría a su querida abuela para ir a vivir con sus padres. Estaba emocionada, pero también triste.

What would she do when she got to America?
How would she live in a new country without speaking
the language?
Would she ever see her grandma again?
And how could she leave her very best friends?

¿Qué iba a hacer al llegar a Norteamérica?
¿Cómo iba a vivir en un país nuevo sin hablar el idioma?
¿Volvería a ver a su abuela otra vez?
Y, ¿cómo podría dejar a sus mejores amigos?

On the last day of summer, Perla and her friends went to play in the forest one last time.

"I can't believe you're really leaving," said Pablo.

Perla felt like crying. "I know. But if this is really our last day together, then let's enjoy it."

En el último día del verano, Perla y sus amigos fueron a jugar en el bosque por última vez.

—No puedo creer que te vayas en serio —dijo Pablo.

Perla sentía que quería llorar.

—Lo sé. Pero si este es de verdad nuestro último día juntos, entonces vamos a disfrutarlo.

"You're right," said Genesis. "Anyone up for hide and seek?"

Perla closed her eyes and started counting down. "10..9..8…" When she reached 1, she started looking for her friends. The forest was so quiet. She couldn't hear anyone, only the birds in the trees and the rushing river nearby.

—Tienes razón —dijo Génesis—. ¿Alguien quiere jugar a las escondidas?

Perla cerró los ojos y empezó a contar:

—10… 9… 8… —Cuando llegó al 1, empezó a buscar a sus amigos.

El bosque estaba tan silencioso. No podía oír a nadie, solo a las aves en los árboles y el río corriendo.

Perla looked everywhere, but she couldn't find her friends. They were really good at hide and seek! She thought she heard footsteps and followed the sound to a bush. But when she pulled back the branches she didn't see her friends. Instead she found a fountain.

Perla buscó en todas partes, pero no podía encontrar a sus amigos. ¡Eran demasiado buenos jugando a las escondidas! Creyó oír pasos y siguió el sonido hacia un arbusto, pero cuando apartó las ramas no vio a sus amigos. En su lugar, encontró una fuente.

"Wow!" said Perla. She called her friends over. "This looks like the magic fountain my grandma used to tell me about it."

"I wonder if it's really magic," said Genesis.

"If it was, what would you wish for?" asked Pablo.

Perla was quiet for a moment. She thought about what she wanted most in the world. "I wish we could make more memories together," she said.

—¡Wow! —exclamó Perla y llamó a sus amigos —Esto se parece a la fuente mágica de la cual mi abuela me hablaba.

—Me pregunto si es realmente mágica —dijo Génesis.

—Si lo fuera, qué deseo pedirías? —preguntó Pablo.

Perla calló un momento. Pensó en lo que más deseaba en el mundo.

—Desearía que pudiéramos crear más recuerdos juntos.

They watched the fountain, hoping for a miracle. But nothing happened.

"I guess we should head back now," said Genesis. Disappointed, they turned towards home.

Suddenly they heard a soft whinny behind them. When they looked back at the fountain, the unicorn statue had come to life!

Los tres velaban la fuente esperando por un milagro. Pero no sucedía nada.

—Supongo que deberíamos volver —dijo Génesis. Decepcionados, se giraron para volver a casa.

De repente escucharon un suave relincho. Cuando se voltearon a ver la fuente, la estatua del unicornio había cobrado vida!

Perla couldn't believe her eyes. A *real* unicorn. She was so excited!

"I heard your wish and I want to help you," said the unicorn. "I will give you three magical memories together."

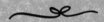

Perla no podía creer lo que veía. Un unicornio *de verdad*. ¡Qué emocionante!

—Escuché tu deseo y quiero ayudarles —dijo el unicornio—. Les daré tres recuerdos mágicos juntos.

Pablo's wish was first.

"I wish for the ultimate soccer match! Us against the other kids in town."

The unicorn bowed and poof! They were standing in a soccer stadium as big as the World Cup, filled with people cheering for Perla and her friends.

The other kids didn't stand a chance. Perla, Genesis, and Pablo were the better players and they won 2-0!

El deseo de Pablo iba primero.

—¡Deseo el mejor partido de fútbol! Nosotros contra los otros niños del pueblo.

El unicornio hizo una reverencia y desapareció. Estaban parados en un estadio de fútbol tan grande como el de la Copa Mundial, lleno de gente animando a Perla y a sus amigos.

Los otros niños no tenían ninguna oportunidad. Perla, Génesis y Pablo fueron los mejores jugadores ¡y ganaron 2-0!

Genesis's wish was next.

"I want the fanciest dinner with all our favorite foods!"

Poof! The stadium around them changed into a beautiful restaurant with an aquarium in the middle and a huge table.

They ate hamburgers, and taquitos, and shrimp pasta, and empanadas, and plantains, and tres leches, and a banana split with caramel drizzled on top.

"This is delicious!" they shouted.

Siguieron por el deseo de Génesis.

—Yo quiero la cena más fina con todas nuestras comidas favoritas.

¡Poof! El estadio en el que estaban se convirtió en un hermoso restaurante con un acuario en el medio y una mesa enorme.

Comieron hamburguesas, y taquitos, y pasta con camarones, y empanadas, y plátanos, y tres leches, y una banana split con chorritos de caramelo arriba.

—¡Está delicioso! —exclamaron.

Perla's wish was last.

"I wish for the most beautiful garden with giant flowers and plants!"

Poof! The restaurant transformed into a lush green garden with daisies as big as Perla's head and watermelons the size of boulders.

The trio played their favorite game of make believe around all the giant plants.

Por último, llegaron al deseo de Perla.

—¡Deseo el jardín más hermoso con flores y plantas gigantes!

¡Puf! El restaurante se transformó en un exuberante jardín verde con margaritas tan grandes como la cabeza de Perla y sandías enormes como peñascos.

El trío jugaba a su juego favorito imaginando fantasías en las plantas gigantes.

By the time they used all their wishes, it was sunset. It was time to go home.

Perla felt heartbroken. She didn't want to say goodbye.

"I guess this is really it," said Pablo. "I'm gonna miss you."

"Me too," said Genesis, teary eyed.

The three of them came in for a group hug before going their separate ways.

Para cuando usaron todos sus deseos, estaba atardeciendo. Ya era hora de ir a casa.

Perla sentía que se le partía el corazón. No quería decir adiós.

—Supongo que esto es todo —dijo Pablo—. Te voy a extrañar.

Yo también —dijo Génesis con ojos llorosos.

Los tres se abrazaron antes de seguir sus caminos.

Perla walked back home still thinking of her friends. *Will they forget about me?*

When she got home, her grandma was waiting for her outside of their house. "What's wrong, mija?"

Perla ran and hugged her grandma. "I'm sad," she said. "I'll miss everyone so much."

Perla caminó de vuelta a casa pensando en sus amigos. *¿Se irán a olvidar de mí?*

Cuando llegó a su casa, su abuela la estaba esperando afuera de su casa.

—¿Qué pasa, mija?

Perla corrió y abrazó a su abuela.

—Estoy triste —le dijo—. Voy a extrañarles tanto a todos.

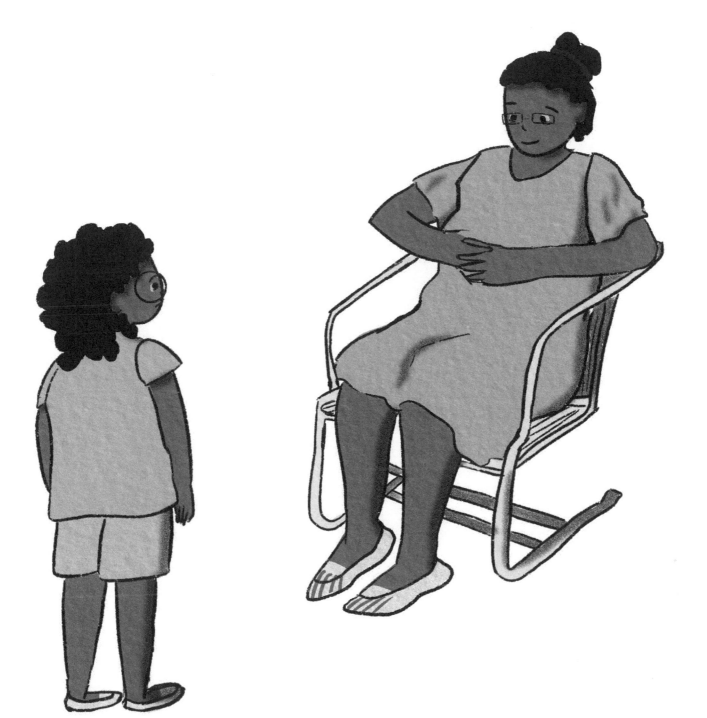

"It's okay to be sad," said her grandma. "But just because you're leaving doesn't mean you'll leave behind your friends."

Perla nodded, trying to believe her. Her eyes welled with tears.

"Oh, my dear," said her grandma. "You carry your friends in your heart! Along with your memories together!"

—No pasa nada por estar triste —dijo su abuela—. Pero el hecho de que te estés yendo no significa que vayas a dejar atrás a tus amigos.

Perla asintió, tratando de creerle. Sus ojos se llenaron de lágrimas.

—Oh, querida —dijo su abuela—. Llevas a tus amigos en el corazón, junto a los recuerdos que tienes con ellos.

Perla and her grandma made their way inside the house. But it was dark inside. Her grandma flicked on the lights.

"Surprise!" shouted everyone.

The whole town was there, even Pablo and Genesis. Perla was so surprised!

"This is for you, mija," said her grandma. "We all love you and we wanted to do something special to send you off."

Perla y su abuela entraron en la casa, pero estaba oscuro adentro. Su abuela encendió las luces.

—¡Sorpresa! —gritaron todos.

El pueblo entero estaba ahí. Incluso Pablo y Génesis. ¡Perla estaba tan sorprendida!

—Esto es para ti, mija —dijo su abuela—. Todos te queremos y queríamos hacer algo especial para despedirnos de ti.

"We have a gift for you, too," said Pablo. "It's from me, Genesis, and the unicorn."

Genesis pulled out a gift-wrapped box. When Perla opened it, a tablet was inside.

"With this we can talk to you every day."

Perla wiped her tears and smiled. "Grandma's right — I will carry all of you with me. You are just the magic I need."

—Te tenemos un regalo también —dijo Pablo—. De parte de Génesis, el Unicornio, y yo.

Génesis sacó una caja envuelta con papel de regalo. Cuando Perla la abrió, encontró una tableta en su interior.

—Con esto podremos hablar contigo todos los días.

Perla se limpió las lágrimas y sonrió.

—Abuela tiene razón: los llevaré a todos conmigo. Ustedes son la magia que necesito.

About the Authors

Deyssy Mosso is 24 years old and a junior in college at the University of the District of Columbia. She is originally from Mexico. Deyssy likes to paint, read, and write, as well as spend time with her little sister. This is her second book with Shout Mouse Press. She is also a co-author of *Voces Sin Fronteras*.

Her favorite part of this process was the imagination it took to brainstorm and create this book. She hopes that kids who read her story understand the importance of keeping friendships strong.

Deyssy Mosso tiene 24 años y está en su tercer año en la Universidad del Distrito de Columbia. Es originaria de México. A Deyssy le gusta pintar, leer y escribir, y también pasar tiempo con su hermana menor. Este es su segundo libro con Shout Mouse Press. También fue coautora del libro Voces sin Fronteras.

Su parte favorita de este proceso fue la imaginación que tomó el proceso de compartir ideas y crearlas. Espera que los niños que lean este cuento entiendan la importancia de mantener fuertes sus amistades.

Faith Campbell served as Story Coach for this book, with **Josselyn Mendoza** supporting.

Yenner Rengifo Chaverra is 15 years old and attends DC International High School. He is originally from Colombia. Yenner enjoys playing soccer, drawing, and spending time with his friends. This is his first book. The whole writing process was fun but his favorite part was meeting the illustrator and seeing the writing come to life. He hopes readers will read this story and want to keep in contact with long distance friends.

Yenner Rengifo Chaverra tiene 15 años y asiste a la Escuela Secundaria Internacional de D.C. Es Colombiano. Le gusta jugar al fútbol, dibujar y pasar tiempo con sus amigos. Este es su primer libro. Todo del proceso de escritura fue divertido, pero su parte favorita fue conocer a la ilustradora y ver como sus escritos cobraron vida. Espera que los lectores lean este cuento y quieran mantenerse en contacto con sus amigos de larga distancia.

Writers and artists at work

ABOUT LAYC

The Latin American Youth Center (LAYC) is a DC-based nonprofit organization that offers a variety of programming to low-income youth of all backgrounds. Their mission is to empower a diverse population of young people to achieve a successful transition to adulthood, through multicultural, comprehensive, and innovative programs that address youths' social, academic, and career needs.

El Latin American Youth Center (LAYC) es una organización sin fines de lucro con sede en Washington, DC que ofrece una variedad de programas para jóvenes de bajos recursos de todos los orígenes. Su misión consiste en capacitar a una población diversa de jóvenes para que logren una transición exitosa a la edad adulta a través de programas multiculturales, integrales e innovadores que abordan las necesidades sociales, académicas y profesionales de la juventud.

Learn more at layc-dc.org

ABOUT SHOUT MOUSE PRESS

Shout Mouse Press is a nonprofit organization dedicated to centering and amplifying the voices of marginalized youth (ages 12+) via writing workshops, publication, and public speaking opportunities. The young people we coach are underrepresented—as characters and as creators—within young people's literature, and their perspectives underheard. Our work provides a platform for them to tell their own stories and, as published authors, to act as leaders and agents of change.

Shout Mouse Press es una organización sin fines de lucro dedicada a centrar y amplificar las voces de los jóvenes marginalizados (a partir de los 12 años) a través de talleres de escritura, publicación, y oportunidades para hablar en público. La gente joven a la que entrenamos está subrepresentada—como personajes y como creadores—en la literatura para gente joven, y sus perspectivas son poco escuchadas. Nuestro trabajo les proporciona una plataforma para contar sus propias historias y, como autores publicados, actuar como líderes y agentes de cambio.

Learn more at shoutmousepress.org

MORE BOOKS FROM SHOUT MOUSE PRESS

Shout Mouse Press is passionate about letting young people speak for themselves—and making sure they are heard. We lead writing and art workshops that center youth voices, then edit and design their books, and finally publish and promote their important work. We ensure that earned income from book sales is invested directly back into young people themselves: proceeds support scholarship funds for author communities, salaries for author interns, and programs that help young people speak up, be heard, and be taken seriously as leaders in their community.

Check out our catalogue of 50+ award-winning youth-authored titles including children's books, graphic novels, novels, memoirs, and poetry collections at **shoutmousepress.org**.

WHERE TO BUY

We encourage you to order books directly through Shout Mouse Press online in order to best benefit our authors. For bulk orders, educator inquiries, and nonprofit discounts: email **orders@shoutmousepress.org**.

Books are also available through Amazon, Bookshop.org, and other online retailers.

Shout Mouse titles are distributed by Ingram.

OTHER WAYS TO ENGAGE

Shout Mouse Press can bring speakers to your class or event. Call us at 240-772-1545 or request via **shoutmousepress.org/ request-an-author-talk**.

Support our youth writing and publishing programs by becoming a donor: **shoutmousepress.org/donate**.

OUR IMPACT

90,000+
Shout Mouse books in circulation

8
National Literary Awards, including 4 Book of the Year Designations

$140,000+
raised in scholarship funds for author communities

20,000+
audience members reached through 100+ Author Talks in schools, libraries, and conferences

20,000+
books donated to young readers in need

VOCES SIN FRONTERAS

As immigrants and activists, the Latino Youth Leadership Council of LAYC recognized the urgent need for #OwnVoices stories to provide a human face to the U.S. immigration debate. With few youth-focused books reflecting their personal narratives, they decided to boldly share their own. The Shout Mouse team of teaching artists and comic coaches worked with these youth leaders to share their memoirs about immigrating to the U.S., and now educators across the country are using their stories to educate, affirm, and inspire their students. For ages 12+.

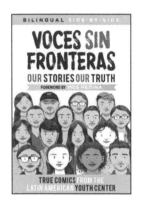

Voces Sin Fronteras: Our Stories, Our Truth
978-1945434921

Voces Sin Fronteras is a bilingual collection of 16 self-illustrated graphic memoirs by teen immigrants from Central America and the Caribbean. These thought-provoking and powerfully honest stories address themes of poverty, family, grief, education, and, of course, the pain and promise of immigration. This book is an opportunity to hear directly from youth who are often in the headlines but whose stories don't get told in full. Foreword by Newbery Medal winner Meg Medina.

"When I tell my story, it heals what it is in my past.... If you never share, the pain will never leave, it will always be there... [Telling your story] will help you to heal inside, to be who you are, to speak out."

— **Erminia**,
co-author of
Voces Sin Fronteras,
on the power of
sharing her story
via Author Talks

REVIEWS

"This powerful compendium amplifies teens' understanding of the young immigrant experience— facing fears, overcoming sadness, learning a new language, and being left by parents who migrated first, then forgiving and reuniting with them decades later... VERDICT: Spotlighting underrepresented voices, this work is highly recommended for all communities in their efforts to promote empathetic, inclusive discussions around immigration."
—*School Library Journal,* Starred Review

"The compelling stories shared by these students… signal their desire to serve as beacons or lifelines for other young immigrants. Their testimonies, as Newbery Medal winner Meg Medina points out in her foreword, are ultimately about courage… Enlightening and inspiring #ownvoices accounts by young activists." — *Kirkus Reviews*

AWARDS

2020 International Latino
Book Awards
Best Young Adult Nonfiction

2019 "In the Margins"
Top Nonfiction Prize

CPSIA information can be obtained
at www.ICGtesting.com
Printed in the USA
LVHW070948080122
708053LV00019B/946